THE Custom ART COLLECTION

Art for the
Contemporary Home

One-of-a-kind artwork *expertly* curated by

A Collection of Frameable, *Original Prints* From Top Artists

Ashley *and* Jamin Mills

The Handmade Home:
Creating a Haven for the Every Day

thehand madehome .net

Adamsmedia
Avon, Massachusetts

Published by
Adams Media, a division of F+W Media, Inc.
57 Littlefield Street, Avon, MA 02322. U.S.A.
www.adamsmedia.com

ISBN 10: 1-4405-7090-6
ISBN 13: 978-1-4405-7090-2

Printed in Mexico.

10 9 8 7 6 5 4 3 2 1

Cover images © Annie Bailey, Stephanie Sliwinski, Robert Scozzari, Ashley Mills, Cassia Beck, Ros Berryman.

This book is available at quantity discounts for bulk purchases.
For information, please call 1-800-289-0963.

Introduction

When you choose something for your home that you truly adore, it speaks to you. It moves you; it sparks something almost inexplicable in your soul. In the search for that gem, you create timeless spaces that tell the story of your life. By juxtaposing items that flow together in your own style, you become the ultimate composer of your spaces.

Now, with the forty inspiring pieces of art found within *The Custom Art Collection: Art for the Contemporary Home*, you'll be able to quickly and easily find that perfect addition to your space; that much-needed, one-of-a-kind creation! This carefully curated, eclectic array of inspiring pieces you'll find throughout are all from incredibly talented photographers, designers, and artists we love. With their participation and generosity, we are able to showcase a glimpse of their creations. Just for you!

Now that you've found pieces that you love, what next? The prints included here will fit any 8" × 10" frame, with limitless possibilities for matting and frame design. The perforated edge makes it easy to remove the images and create your own art gallery in just minutes!

When it comes to using art in your home, there are a lot of different opinions out there, and sometimes all those voices can be a little overwhelming. We believe, first and foremost, that you should do what feels right to you. But what do you do when in doubt? Here are three main categories we stick to when it comes to grouping art.

1. Color

- **Create Depth:** Use pieces that have varying shades in the same tones to create depth and interest on your walls. Consider this strategy with both frames and art. The frames are just as important, so let them work together to hold something beautiful on those walls.
- **Play with Contrast:** Think in terms of opposites and try to balance them. Bringing in an element like a metal frame and juxtaposing it with natural wood, or traditional art with

contemporary can create a beautiful look all on its own.

- **Freshen Up:** When searching for the perfect frames to group together, don't forget to scout sales racks at home design stores for interesting shapes. Or even try shopping the rooms of your own home for a new spin on a forgotten piece. You can bring new life to old frames by unifying them with varying shades of the same color. This applies to the matte in a frame, too. Don't let a blah color hold you back. Give it a spritz with spray paint; add stripes with painter's tape; or use a stencil for a bold, unexpected statement.

2. Numbers

- **Odd Numbers:** When dealing with groupings, odd numbers are known to play with the eye to create a more appealing display.

- **Even Numbers:** If you prefer symmetry on your walls, try even-numbered groupings. Always use pairings or equal numbers when going for a bold, simplistic statement, and a cleaner look.

- **Ratio:** When using frames together, remember this: One large frame paired with two smaller ones makes a great balanced look, even when working with odd numbers. Always consider this element in your groupings.

3. Display

- **Always at Eye Level:** The most common mistake we see is hanging art too high. Strive for eye level. When hanging frames in groups, always go for a spacing that keeps them closer, with the negative space greater on the outsides than in between.

- **Hanging over Furniture:** Keep frames and art no higher than 5 to 6 inches above a piece of furniture for a clean, intentional look.

- **Practice Makes Perfect:** Hanging things on the wall can sometimes feel laborious and downright intimidating. Don't be afraid to sketch it out for proportions, lay it on the floor, and measure. Cut pieces of paper to size and tape them to the wall to try it out. Ask your friends for another opinion. Small holes in walls are pretty forgiving in the grand scheme of things, so even if you mess up, there's a fix for that.

Above all, be brave, stay flexible, and just go for it. This is how we grow, learn, and create personal displays of beautiful, one-of-a-kind art in our homes!

It is our hope that, within the pages of this book, you find inspiration. If you're looking for your voice or maybe even a springboard to cultivate your home into a reflection of who you really are, we hope that you find something you're crazy about, let go of your fears, and love the home you create. And if you're looking for more design options or need help arranging these beautiful images, take a look at *Handmade Walls*, *The Custom Art Collection: Art for the Traditional Home*, and *The Custom Art Collection: Art for the Eclectic Home*, the companions to this title.

The walls of your home hold the potential for great beauty and we hope you feel passionate about the possibilities for beauty that lie within. After all, when you add something that speaks to you, it truly can take your space to an entirely different level of amazing. Art is the perfect place to begin . . . the ultimate inspiration.

Ashley *and* **Jamin Mills**

The Handmade Home:
Creating a Haven for the Every Day

thehand
madehome
.net

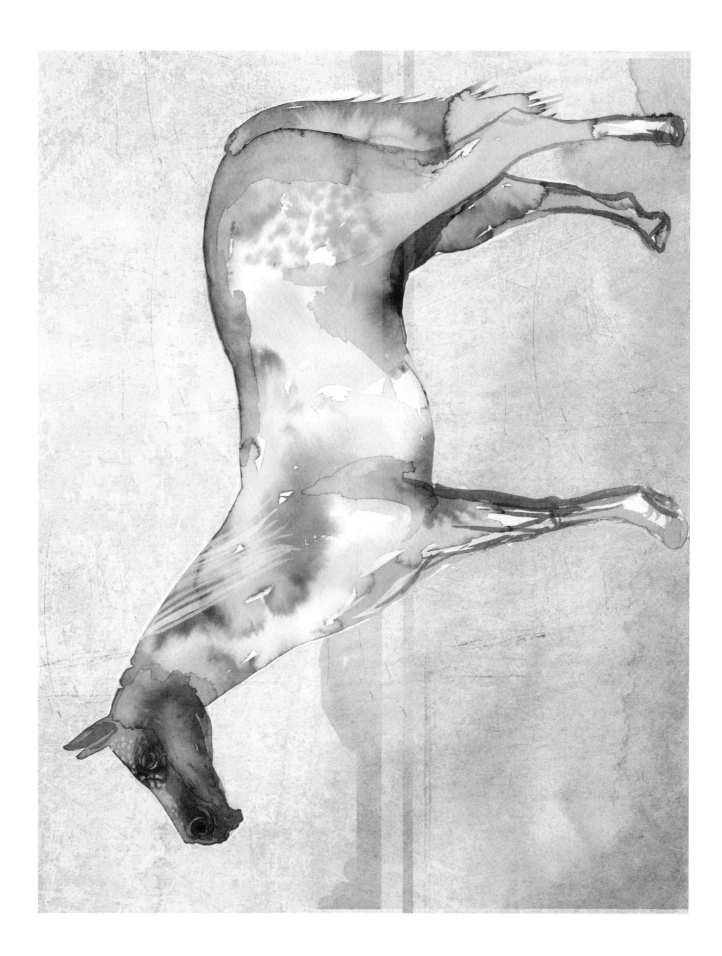

Courtney Oquist
"Horse"

Jan Skácelík
"Abs 2"

Ashley Percival
"Boating"

Beth Wold
"Humpback Whale"

Brandy Cattoor
"Behind the City of Craig"

Ashley Mills
"Colorado Sky"

Ros Berryman
"Spring Light"

Cassia Beck
"Honeycomb II"

Beth Wold
"Ladybug on a Pink Dahlia"

Annie Bailey
"The Green Ladder"

Carolyn Finnell
"On the Road"

Carolyn Finnell
"Legendary"

Carolyn Finnell
"The Kiss"

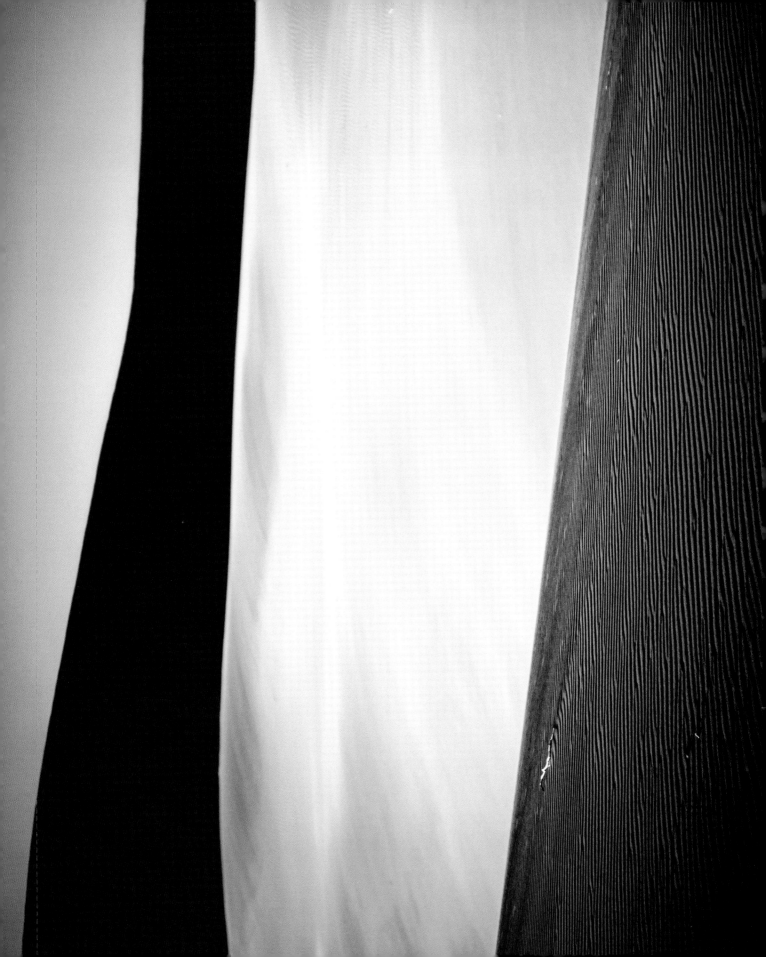

Beth Wold
"Namib VIII"

Christine Lindstrom
"Fragile"

Christine Wiemers
"Right to the Wall"

Courtney Oquist
"GeoCloud"

Laura Prill
"Black and White Crossword Weaving"

Jenny Gray
"Detail No. 2"

Courtney Oquist
"What You Talking About"

Beth Wold
"Wild Horse IV"

Marianne LoMonaco
"Let's Get Lost"

Yellena James
"Spurt"

Brandy Cattoor
"Red Shack"

Ros Berryman
"Amber Moon"

L. Claudine Song
"Upbeat"

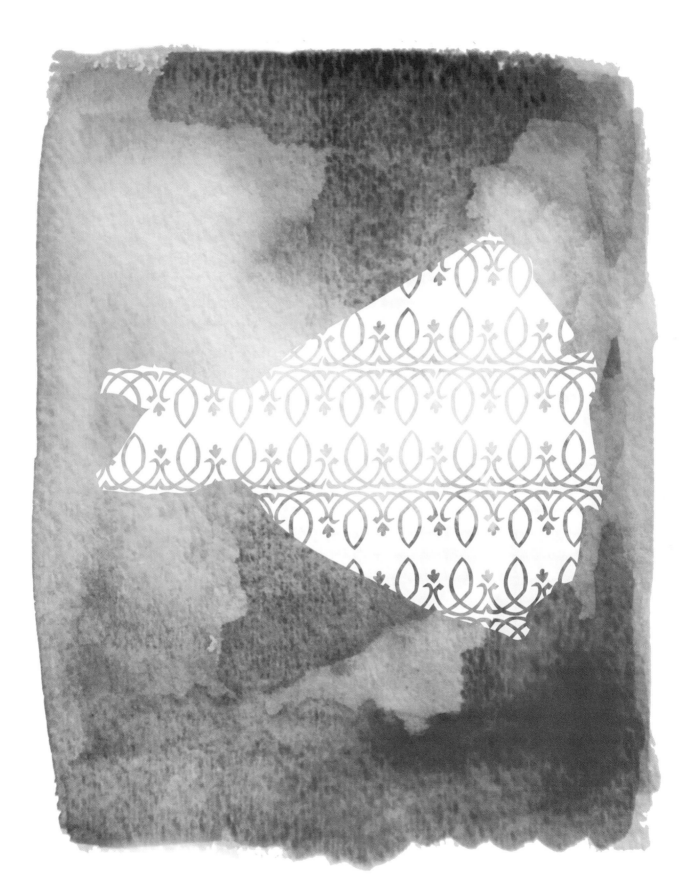

Ashley Mills
"Dress"

Jianping Yi
"Landscape #9"

Rachel Bingaman
"Today's Embrace"

Robert Scozzari
"Origami 29"

Christine Wiemers
"Urban Geometry"

Linda Donohue
"Coastal Whisper"

Ashley Mills
"Sweetheart"

Sarah B. Martinez
"Field No. 3"

Sarah B. Martinez
"Colored Mountain"

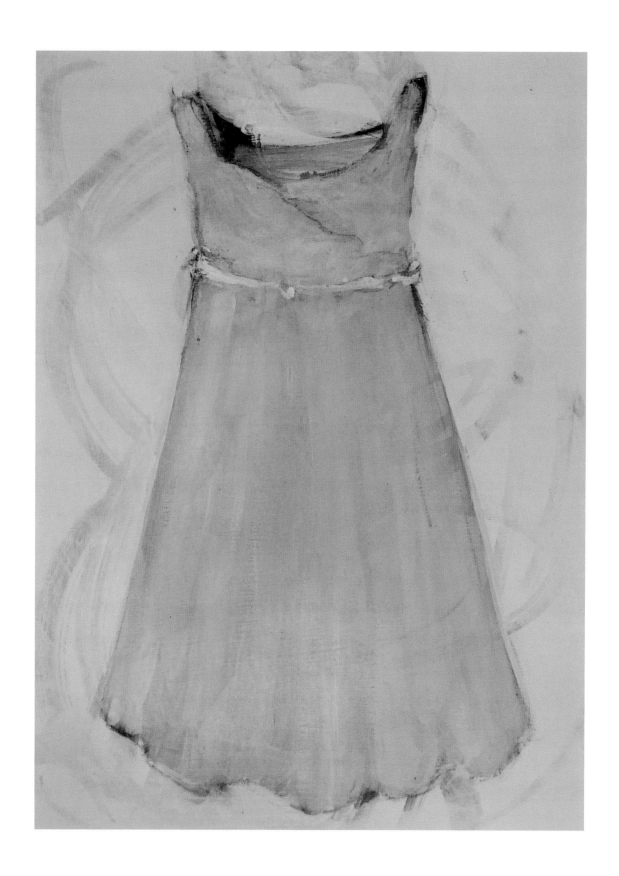

Shannon Lewis
"Yellow Dress #2"

Stephanie Sliwinski
"Navajo Inspired Arrows"

Sonja Caldwell
"Japanese Parasol"

Credits

Annie Bailey, *Montana Photo Journal*
"Little Lovely"
"The Green Ladder"
www.mtphotojournal.etsy.com
Annie Bailey is the photographer for *Montana Photo Journal*. Her work is a reflection of a life spent surrounded by open space and blue sky. She was born and raised in Montana, with most of her life spent on her family's ranch in the Smith River valley. Seeing and documenting the tiny moments in life is what she wants to do for the rest of her life.

Cassia Beck, *Violet May Collage*
"Honeycomb II"
www.CassiaBeck.com
Cassia Beck is an artist and photographer from Brighton, UK. She creates artwork inspired by vintage book covers, midcentury advertising, and design. Cassia uses vintage magazines, cut paper, and her own photography to create tongue-in-cheek scenarios with a vintage edge.

Ros Berryman
"Spring Light"
"Amber Moon"
Fizzstudio.co.uk
Born and living in England, Ros Berryman gained a BA (Honors) in graphic design and then went on to set up a small design company publishing greeting cards. Wanting to have more artistic freedom, she is now also making fine art prints of her work. Inspired by her love of nature and of working with digital photography, (with carefully considered post editing), she hopes to inject a little magic into each image.

Rachel Bingaman, *Bing Art*
"Today's Embrace"
www.etsy.com/shop/BingArt
Rachel Bingaman lives in the Washington, D.C. area with her husband and two children. She launched her professional career as an artist in January 2012. She comes from an artistic family and her favorite medium is oil. Her current artistic focus mainly revolves around abstract realism and contemporary landscapes. Rachel's inspiration comes from a variety of sources, but the inspiration she finds in the unsurpassed beauty of nature is what drives her palette.

Sonja Caldwell
"Japanese Parasol"
www.etsy.com/shop/sonjacaldwell
Sonja was born in Kansas but moved to Japan at age 7, then to California at age 10. She holds a BA in studio art from UC Davis. Being the daughter of a wanderlust and an international businessman, she has always enjoyed travel photography and has had a lot of opportunities to do it. As a photographer, her main subject is Paris, France. She splits her time between Paris and her home in San Jose, California.

Brandy Cattoor
"Behind the City of Craig"
"Red Shack"
www.BrandyCattoor.com
Brandy Cattoor graduated with a BFA in oil painting from Brigham Young University Idaho in 2011. She has completed commission work for drawings and oil paintings. She is interested in architectural landscapes, cityscapes, still lifes, and portraiture. Along with oil painting, Brandy creates and sells handmade paper products. Eventually she hopes to merge both creative forms into one.

Linda Donohue, *Linda Donohue Fine Art*
"Coastal Whisper"
www.LPDart.com
Linda Donohue grew up at Muir Beach, just North of the Golden Gate and in the Napa Valley. Impressions of northern California and her continued passion for riding are the inspirations for Donohue's paintings. She paints abstract seascapes, cities and horses in acrylics with a pallet knife, and also paints in ink. Her paintings are in collections throughout the world and sold through galleries, art festivals, Etsy.com, and the High Point and Atlanta Furniture Markets.

Carolyn Finnell
"On the Road"
"Legendary"
"The Kiss"
www.FinnellFineArt.etsy.com
Carolyn Finnell strives for an intuitive and expressive abstraction of nature and emotion. She aims to communicate attitude and personality and to establish a connection with the viewer using only color and form. Carolyn revels in the tension between order and chaos and the battle between reverence and irreverence that occurs in every piece. She paints from the inside out, always seeking the balance of deliberation and spontaneity.

Jenny Gray
"At Rest"
"Detail No. 2"
www.JennyGrayArt.com
Jenny Gray often starts a painting with marks or colors representing specific emotions, places, or people. Then she takes this raw "information" and adds, subtracts, covers, and layers. She likes exploring layers and the tension of knowing something is underneath but not knowing it fully. She creates very much on a gut-level; her paintings are improvised with a head full of remembered feelings and images.

Yellena James
"Spurt"
www.Yellena.com
Yellena James grew up and attended art school in Sarajevo before moving to Portland, Oregon. Each intimate world she creates seems to posses its own ethos and its own special ability to radiate emotion. Her work explores intricate and delicate forms of an imaginary ecosystem, creating an ethereal place that is hauntingly familiar and yet hypnotically exotic. She's done illustrations for many high-profile companies and has done gallery shows around the globe.

Shannon Lewis
"Yellow Dress #2"
www.etsy.com/shop/abstracthome?ref=l2-shop-info-name
Shannon Lewis is a long-term resident of Portland, Oregon and a PSU graduate with a major in fine art. She loves painting, art, her family, friends, and, of course, her cats. Although, her work ranges from large abstracts to small prints, the dress is very special to her. This sweet image evokes a time of childhood parties, first dates, dancing, and joy. Shannon's mixed media dresses are handmade and come in many different colors.

Christine Lindstrom
"Fragile"
Shop.maiautumn.com
In 2009, Christine Lindstrom started her company, Mai Autumn, with the idea of making life a little more beautiful. She believes in savoring the small pleasures in life, lingering, exploring, and being surrounded by inspiring things. She was raised at the Jersey Shore and enjoys cooking, gardening, and reading many, many books, all of which inspire her art greatly. She received her BA in painting in

2008 and is currently living in Ocean Grove, NJ.

Marianne LoMonaco
"Let's Get Lost"
www.MarianneLoMonaco.etsy.com
Marianne LoMonaco is a Toronto-born photographer. She is completely self-taught and in 2009, she finally upgraded her camera to one that actually worked. And fell in love. Hard and fast. Passionately in love. With photography. Completely driven to improve both creatively and technically, never satisfied for long without challenging herself. "It was that year I found a part of my life I was always meant to live."

Sarah B. Martinez
"Field No. 3"
"Colored Mountain"
SarahBMartinez.com
After saying "goodbye" to city life and moving to the country in 2011, Sarah Martinez has brought her daydreams of becoming a flourishing artist to life. She, her musician husband, and their tiny baby moved into a magical stone house in the Northwest hills of Connecticut, where she now muses from her sunny home studio. Along with earth and sky, the flora and fauna in between are her sweetest inspirations.

Ashley Mills
"Colorado Sky"
"Dress"
"Sweetheart"
www.thehandmadehome.net
Ashley mixes her love of art, great design, and writing into full-time fun at Thehand madehome.net. Here you'll find stories on a little bit of everything from the fun of parenthood to a love for everyday life.

Laura Prill
"Black and White Crossword Weaving"
www.lauraprill.etsy.com
Colorado-based with New York roots, artist Laura Prill is a signature member of the Colorado Watercolor Society and is a published illustrator. She relishes the technical challenge of making realistic art and the imaginative wrestling of creating abstract collages with hidden details and words that bring the viewer closer. Nothing is wasted, as her paper weavings are formed from the precious remnants of old and new work. She runs several online shops and is the President of Heartworks Inc. Laura has recorded two solo piano CDs and others with her husband, Brad.

Courtney Oquist
"Horse"
"What You Talking About"
"GeoCloud"
www.courtneyoquist.etsy.com
Courtney Oquist is an artist and art teacher based in Huntington Beach, CA. Through painting and drawing, Courtney explores the fantastical and eccentric part of everydayness. She is inspired by nature, by people, by beauty, and especially by color and the meditative act of painting.

Ashley Percival
"Boating"
www.etsy.com/uk/shop/
AshleyPercival?ref=si_shop
Ashley Percival is a freelance illustrator from England. His artwork is suitable for all ages and has been described as fun, unique, and quirky. He has had his art licensed for a range of products including home decor, wall art, clothing, stationery, and watches.

Robert Scozzari
"Origami 29"
www.ArtsyDesigny.com
What if Jackson Pollock or Mark Rothko owned a Mac? This is a question Canadian artist and graphic designer Robert Scozzari asks. After 18 years as a graphic designer, Robert followed his heart, and by combining his skills as a designer with his love for modern art, he created his own unique style. "I create art that I love to see, having fun and loving every minute of it. You should do the same!"

Jan Skácelík
"Abs 2"
www.etsy.com/shop/handz
Jan Skácelík is a graphic designer from Olomouc, a small city in the Czech Republic. After studying graphic design, she worked in many graphic studios until finally her passion for Scandinavian design, mid century modern, and pop culture design brought her to making her retro-inspired art prints.

L. Claudine Song
"Upbeat"
www.ClaudineSongArt.com
Claudine Song's work is fueled by her interest in creating colorful abstracts where "everything is possible." She creates abstracts that vibrate with life and are on the verge of movement and change. In each piece, she explores the chaotic with a sense of balance and whimsy. She was born in 1963 in Ithaca, New York and graduated from the University of Southern California.

Christine Wiemers, 9th Cycle Studios
"Right to the Wall"
"Urban Geometry"
www.etsy.com/shop/9thCycleStudios
Born in Toowoomba, Australia in 1979, Christine Wiemers received her first camera as a preteen and was fascinated with capturing the details of particular moments in life. This appeal continued through the years as she continued learning about and honing her craft. With the advent of Photoshop, she's found new ways to showcase her stylish atmosphere. Christine moved to San Francisco in 2006, where she now focuses on both nature and contemporary society.

Beth Wold
"Humpback Whale"
"Namib VIII"
"Ladybug on a Pink Dahlia"
"Wild Horse IV"
www.bethwold.com
Beth Wold is a fine art photographer specializing in landscape and wildlife photography. Beth is a North Dakota resident who spent 17 years in Africa, where her passion for wild places and wild things was ignited. Beth earned her BA in photography at the University of North Dakota.

Jianping Yi
"Landscape #9"
www.saatchionline.com/jp_yi
Jianping Yi, born 1957, is a famous landscape painter. He lives in Beijing, China and Arizona, USA.

Stephanie Sliwinski,
Fancy That Design House & Co.
"Navajo Inspired Arrows"
www.fancythatdesignhouse.etsy.com
Stephanie Sliwinski is owner/designer of Fancy That Design House & Co., near Milwaukee, WI. Her childhood love of drawing rainbows and unicorns led her to a degree in both art and graphic communication. Upon graduation, she worked full time, creating apparel graphics for a wide variety of national retail accounts. These days, she is wife to an amazingly supportive husband, Chad, and mother of two young boys, Colton & Beckham. When she is not playing superheroes or stepping on Legos, she can be found designing graphics full of elements she loves—color, texture, typography, and personal meaning.

Acknowledgments

To the amazingly talented artists who were gracious enough to share their beautiful creations with all of us: thank you. This book would not be possible without you.

To the wonderful team at Adams Media for their insight, patience, and seeing something in us, we are so humbled. You have been a delight.

And to our inspiring readers, we are forever awed and grateful for all of you.

Thank you.

About the Authors

Jamin and Ashley Mills began their adventure together as college sweethearts. After a decade of marriage and three offspring later, they currently reside with their family in Montgomery, Alabama. They are the voices behind this book and their website, *www.thehandmadehome.net*.

At The Handmade Home, they share their daily journey and down-to-earth passion as the parents to three incredible children and one crazy dog. In between the mountainous piles of dirty laundry and musical bed fiascos with their glorious little troublemakers, they're also known for their handmade revamps and one-of-a-kind projects as they create a haven for the everyday.

For more inspiring projects and one-of-a-kind creations, visit The Handmade Home at *www.thehandmadehome.net*.

Ashley *and* Jamin Mills
The Handmade Home:
Creating a Haven for the Every Day

thehand madehome .net

Bid farewell to blank walls and say hello to the art you love—all at an exceptional value.

The Custom Art Collection makes it easy and inexpensive for you to find the perfect print for every corner of your home. Featuring curated collections for contemporary, eclectic, and traditional homes, each book in this lovely series showcases original artwork from up-and-coming artists and pairs the prints with others in the collection to complete the look.

Art for the Eclectic Home
Trade Paperback
978-1-4405-7089-6, $22.99

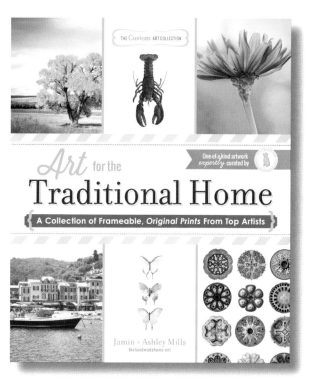

Art for the Traditional Home
Trade Paperback
978-1-4405-7088-9, $22.99

Beautiful DIY Décor for a One-of-a-Kind Home

Perfect for those who want to fill their space with unique personality, *Handmade Walls* offers 22 fabulous DIY projects—each easy enough to achieve in a day. Get that creative look you've always wanted without spending a fortune or succumbing to cookie-cutter designs. Your dream home design is within reach!

Available December 18, 2013!

Handmade Walls
Trade Paperback
978-1-4405-7232-6, $24.99